Pry

Ben

Boo

Whoops

Tad

Gnome

This Bill and Ben Annual belongs to...

ManVeer maan

First published in 2001 by BBC Worldwide Ltd, Woodlands, 80 Wood Lane, London, W12 0TT.
Text, design and illustrations © 2001 BBC Worldwide Ltd.
Bill and Ben logo and characters are trademarks of the British Broadcasting Corporation/Ben Productions LLC and are used under licence by BBC Worldwide Ltd. Photographic images, Bill and Ben logo and characters © BBC Worldwide Ltd/Ben Productions LLC 2000. Text, design and original artwork illustrations
© BBC Worldwide Limited 2000. A BBC Worldwide/Ben Productions production, produced by Cosgrove Hall.
© BBC Worldwide Limited/Ben Productions LLC 2000. ISBN 0 563 47670 2.
Written and edited by Andrea Wickstead and Sarah O'Neill.
Art Editor, Susan Jackman. Makes by Susan Jackman.
Colour origination by Polestar Digital Watford Ltd, Watford.
Printed and bound by Proost Nv, Turnhout, Belgium.
Photography by Christopher Baines and Bruce Coleman Ltd. Illustrated by Bill Titcombe, David Crossley,
Jo Davies, Cathy Baxter, Emma Holt, Lorna Kent and Steve Smallman.
A big thank you to Danny, Hayley, Zoe, Sam, Oliver, Felix and Tashana who all appear in this Annual!

Ben Productions LLC

BBC

Flobbadob Fun!

"You are a silly pair!"

Big Time Band

It was a beautiful morning at the bottom of the garden and Bill and Ben were just waking up from their night's sleep.

"Flubbaweed," said Ben, rubbing his eyes.

"Flobbaweed," said Bill, as they looked at Weed. She looked very unhappy.

"I'm sorry, I'm just feeling down in the dumps," sighed Weed, miserably, as her petals hung down around her face.

"Flobbadob?" Bill asked what was wrong.

"Oh, nothing really. It's just that sometimes I'd like to get about a bit more..." said Weed, longingly. "I know I have a happy time here, sitting in the sun and drinking up the rain, but it would be nice to have a little excitement just once in a while..."

Bill and Ben looked at each other, then tried to think of ways to cheer her up. They tried to make Weed smile by jumping and dancing about in front of her.

"Flobadaaaaa!" said Bill, as he landed in front of Weed, after performing a somersault.

"Hiypahh!" cried Ben, as he did a cartwheel. Bill was very impressed by this, but Weed was still unhappy – they hadn't made her feel any better. So they went in search of advice. The Flowerpot Men thought Slowcoach could suggest something that might make Weed feel a little happier.

"Flobbalob Slogachog," said Bill, outside Slowcoach's home. Slowcoach soon poked his head outside.

"Who's out there, making all that noise?" said Slowcoach. "Oh, I should have guessed it was you two."

Bill and Ben explained how unhappy Weed was and asked Slowcoach if he knew what to do. "Who do you think I am? The happiness pixie?" grumbled Slowcoach. "Now clear off, the pair of you..."

As they walked away, they noticed Whimsy the spider's cobweb glistening in the sunlight. "Oh, flubbalub," said Ben, as they went to take a closer look.

They started lightly plucking at the web – 'ping, ping, ping' it went. Suddenly, Whimsy appeared at the top of the web.

"I say, would you mind not doing that?" said Whimsy, who was trying to catch flies in her web. "You'll scare off the flies with all that pinging!"

But this had given Bill an idea to cheer up Weed. He asked Whimsy to spin another web closer to Weed so she could hear the pretty noise.

"Well, I suppose so..." agreed Whimsy.

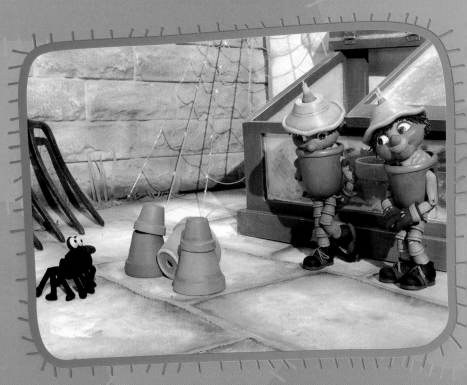

That got Bill and Ben thinking about other things which make interesting sounds. They decided to go off in search of noisy objects which might cheer up Weed.

"Flobbadob!" said Bill, as he dragged Ben over to the potting shed to look for more sounds.

They found some dusters and gardening gloves, but they didn't make much noise! They were about to give up when Ben kicked a small pot of paint over. The pot rolled into another paint pot – CLANG – which then rolled over – CLANK – and knocked some seed packets off the shelf – RATTLE. The last packet then knocked a fork off the shelf – BOING – which landed and bounced around a group of jars and a jug – PLINK PLONK PLINK! Bill and Ben looked at each other in delight. It was music to their ears!

Bill picked up a jug, hoping there might be something musical inside, but there didn't seem to be anything in there but dust.

"Aaaaaahchoooo!" sneezed Bill, as the dust tickled his nose. The echo of his sneeze in the jug, made a deep musical sound!

Ben had been rooting around looking for more sounds when he found a small piece of cane and a paintbrush. He pushed the brush up one end of the cane and blew into the other end, moving the brush back and forth. This made a great whistling noise – FWWWWWEEEEEEE!

"Hee, hee, flobberly!" said Bill, having a go.

"Flobbaweed!" cried Bill, hoping this would cheer Weed up.

They gathered up all the instruments they had found and put them into a sack to take back to Weed.

When they returned, Whimsy had just finished spinning a web next to Weed.

The Flowerpot Men put down their sacks and waved hello to Weed, but she still looked very miserable.

"What have you got there?" she asked Bill and Ben, peering round to look at them.

8

Bill pulled out the jug that made the deep noise, then the fork and jars, the packet of seeds and the paint pots. While Ben showed her his clever whistle.

"What are you going to do with all those?" asked Weed.

"Aahhhh, flobbadob!" said Bill, asking Weed to be patient.

The Flowerpot Men checked that Whimsy was ready to play her web. She was, and they all began to play their instruments at once – just like a real band!

Bill was blowing into the jug and tapping the jars with the fork, then stopping to shake the seed packet and clink the paint pots together, while Ben played a tune on his whistle.

Meanwhile, Whimsy plucked away in harmony at her web, making a lovely strumming sound, in time with Bill and Ben.

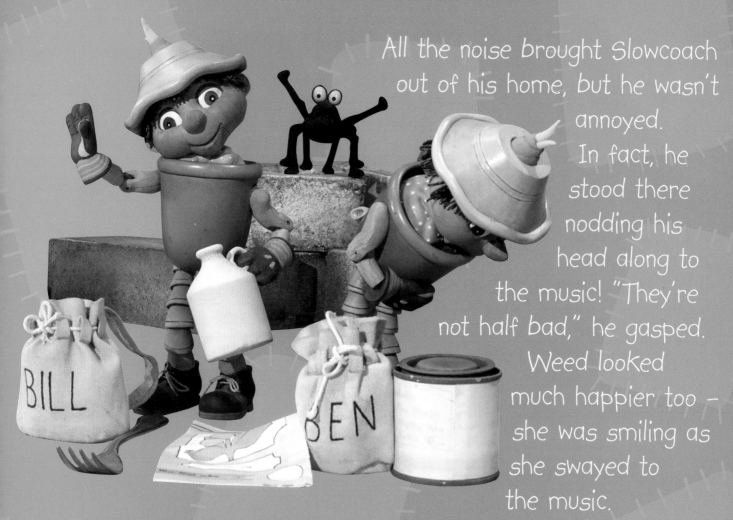

All the noise brought Slowcoach out of his home, but he wasn't annoyed.

In fact, he stood there nodding his head along to the music! "They're not half *bad*," he gasped. Weed looked much happier too – she was smiling as she swayed to the music.

Boo, Whoops and Scamper heard the band playing and hurried over to listen. Next door, Rose and her Buds could hear the music and started swaying, while Tad hopped over in time to the beat. Pry swooped down from her tree and listened from the top of the fence.

"One, two, one two three four: Flobbadob, flobbadob, flobbadob... flobbadobadobadoba Weeeeeed! Flobbadob, flobbadob, flobbadob, flobbadobadobadoba Weeed!" sang Bill and Ben, in time with the music.

When the band had finished playing, everyone cheered.

"Oh, that was lovely!" smiled Weed in delight.

Bill, Ben and Whimsy bowed to their audience. They were very pleased that they had gone down *so* well and that Weed was smiling again.

"Let's play it again!" said Whimsy, counting them in.

"One, two, three, four..."
So the band played their special music again, while Slowcoach, Pry, Whoops, Tad, Boo and Scamper all tapped their feet along in time.

They all loved Bill and Ben's Big Time Band, but no one loved them more than Weed, who knew they had done it just for her!

Home-made band!

Bill and Ben and their friends made their own band. Why don't you make a band with some of your friends? You could put on a concert just like the Big Time Band!

You will need: ♫ card or a cardboard tube ♫ an empty plastic bottle ♫ rice ♫ an old sweet tin

Hayley has rolled up a piece of card into a trumpet shape. When she blows through it, it makes a loud TOOT sound!

TOOOT!

Shhhhshhhhshhh!

Shhhhshhhhshhh!

Danny has made a shaker from an empty plastic bottle and rice. He decorated the bottle with sticky shapes. When he shakes the bottle it goes...
Shhhhshhhhshhh!

BILL

Zoe covered a big sweet tin in foil and paper, then she used two wooden spoons to bang it. BANG BANG!

All together now, one... two... three...

TOOOT!

BANG BANG!

SHHHSHHHSHHH!

13

Colouring - in

Garden friends

Look carefully at the photographs on the opposite page.
Can you match them to Tad, Whimsy, Boo, Slowcoach and Scamper?

1

I can spin lovely webs, just like this one!

2

I can roll up into a prickly ball to protect myself.

3

I love eating tasty nuts and jumping through the branches of trees.

4

I catch my dinner with my long tongue.

5

I move very slowly because I carry my home around on my back!

Have you managed to match the photographs to Bill and Ben's garden friends? Write the numbers in the boxes!

Tad's friend is number

Whimsy's friend is number

Boo's friend is number

Slowcoach's friend is number

Scamper's friend is number

Egg box Slowcoach!

To make Slowcoach, you will need: ◗ Two egg boxes ◗ paints ◗ safe glue ◗ round-ended scissors ◗ modelling clay

1

Carefully cut out the two egg holders in the centre of the first egg box, leaving four for Slowcoach's legs. Stick one of the individual egg holders onto the front of the egg box, to make Slowcoach's head. Now, cut off the lid of the second egg box and glue it on the top to make the shell!

2

Now your Slowcoach is ready to be painted!

18

3

Roll out a piece of clay or plasticine to make a tail and eyes. Then press some small, flat circles of clay for the markings on his face and feet.

"D'you know what? That's not half bad!"

A sun hat for Weed

 and  woke up one morning to find the shining.

"Flubbaphew!" cried Ben. "Flobbadobasun!" cried Bill. It was very

warm in the sunshine. Poor was especially hot, her

petals and were wilting. Bill had an idea, "Robodobolat!"

he cried. "A ?" said Weed. "That would keep me cool."

So  and  went off to find one. They looked everywhere.

In the potting shed, inside a , behind the . They

asked and  and even if they had seen

one, but it was no good. So they went next door. didn't

look very happy when they asked her if she had a .

"No I haven't!" she snapped. "But there is all this  making

sun   Weed   leaves

Bill   Ben   sun hat   flowerpot   watering can

the garden look a mess!" she sniffed, pointing to the paper.

That gave  an idea. "Robodobolat!" he cried. They took

the paper back to and put it on her head, but it kept

falling off. So Ben folded the paper. It took a few tries, but soon

he folded it into a  ! Weed balanced it on her

head – it shaded her from the perfectly. She was much

cooler now and all thanks to those clever Men!

Beautiful Rose

Rose wants to tell you how to make a beautiful flower, just like herself.
You will need: a long green stick   red and green tissue paper
round-ended scissors   sticky tape

1

Cut out some circles and petal shapes from the tissue paper just as Zoe is doing.

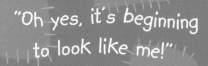

"Oh yes, it's beginning to look like me!"

2

Make small holes in the centre of the tissue paper circles and push them onto the stick, taping them down. These are Rose's pretty petals.

3

When you have pushed all the petals onto the stick, twist the ones in the centre until they look like Rose's face!

"Oh, it's simply marvellous, and almost as beautiful as me!"

4

Finally, add the green leaves and a few different shaped petals around the top and Rose is ready!

Who will you give your Rose to?

23

In the potting shed...

Bill and Ben are looking for useful things in the potting shed. Can you help them find the things on their list? Put a tick in each box as you find them.

What other useful things can you spot in the potting shed?

string for tying up

paintbrush for painting

cotton reel for rolling

pretty seed packet to show Weed

china jug to make a noise with

shiny fork to show Pry

Green fingers

Ketchup knows all about how plants grow. He lives in a greenhouse where all sorts of plants, fruit and vegetables grow. He's telling Bill all about planting. Here are his tips for growing things at home. Why don't you try to grow something?

Cress seeds are really simple to grow!

Cress seeds can be grown indoors, all year round. You can buy cress seeds in most supermarkets or garden centres.

1 Moisten either a piece of cotton wool or paper tissues and sprinkle the seeds on top. Ben has sprinkled his in the shape of his name!

2 Cover the seeds with paper until the seeds start to shoot.

3 Remove the paper and place the seedlings on the windowsill.

4 Once the plants have grown to about 5cm tall, ask an adult to help you harvest them, by cutting the plants with scissors.

Grow a tomato plant, just like Ketchup!

These baby tomato plants can be grown in a pot or a tub.
You will need: ● Dwarf variety of tomato seeds
● compost ● a flowerpot ● bamboo cane

1 It is best to sow the seeds in March or April. Fill the flowerpot with compost and place the seeds under a thin layer of compost at the top. Make sure the soil is moist but not too wet.

2 You should see some little shoots after about a week. When the shoots appear, move the pot to a really sunny windowsill. Remove the weaker seedlings to leave one. Bring the seedlings into a warm room at night, away from any draughts.

3 When the seedling has grown to 7cm tall you should move it to a bigger pot to allow the roots to grow.

4 Remember to keep the soil moist and feed the plant with a tomato feed. When the plant grows bigger, you will need to tie it to a bamboo cane for support.

5 When the weather is warmer, you can stand the plant outside in a sunny spot. In July or August, you will have some tasty tomatoes!

27

Scamper's nutty Search!

Scamper is collecting her winter store of nuts.
There are 10 nuts hidden in this picture.
Can you help her find them all?

Pry's collection boxes

Pry loves collecting shiny things! Do you collect anything?
Why not make these great boxes to show off your collections?
You will need: ☁ a small box (washing powder tablet boxes are best)
☁ paint or paper ☁ safe glue or sticky tape ☁ round-ended scissors

Cut the lid off of the box and stick it inside to make a shelf. You could use other bits of card to make more shelves or compartments!

Paint the box using your favourite colours or cover it in coloured paper.

When the paint has dried, fill the box with your favourite things. Tashana is making this box for Bill and Ben. What has Pry put in her box?

"Shiny treasure!"

Weed's box

Pry's box

Bill and Ben's box

31

Colouring-in

Weed sees the world

"COUGH, COUGH!" went Weed, one morning. She had woken to find the garden full of dust. "Flobbalobadoff?" asked Bill.

"Yes, I did cough," sighed Weed. "There's not been much rain lately, so the garden's very dusty, cough, cough!" she spluttered.

Ben looked at his dusty hands and agreed. "PAH! OOOH! Flubbalubadust!" he cried.

"We need to clean up the dust, Ben. We need a duster..." began Weed, but Ben didn't know what a duster was.

"Lubaluster?" he asked, looking rather confused.

"A duster is a cloth for cleaning things," explained Weed.

Bill and Ben thought they had seen some dusters in the shed, so they sped off to find them. They soon found the dusters and promptly dusted each other down until they were clean again.

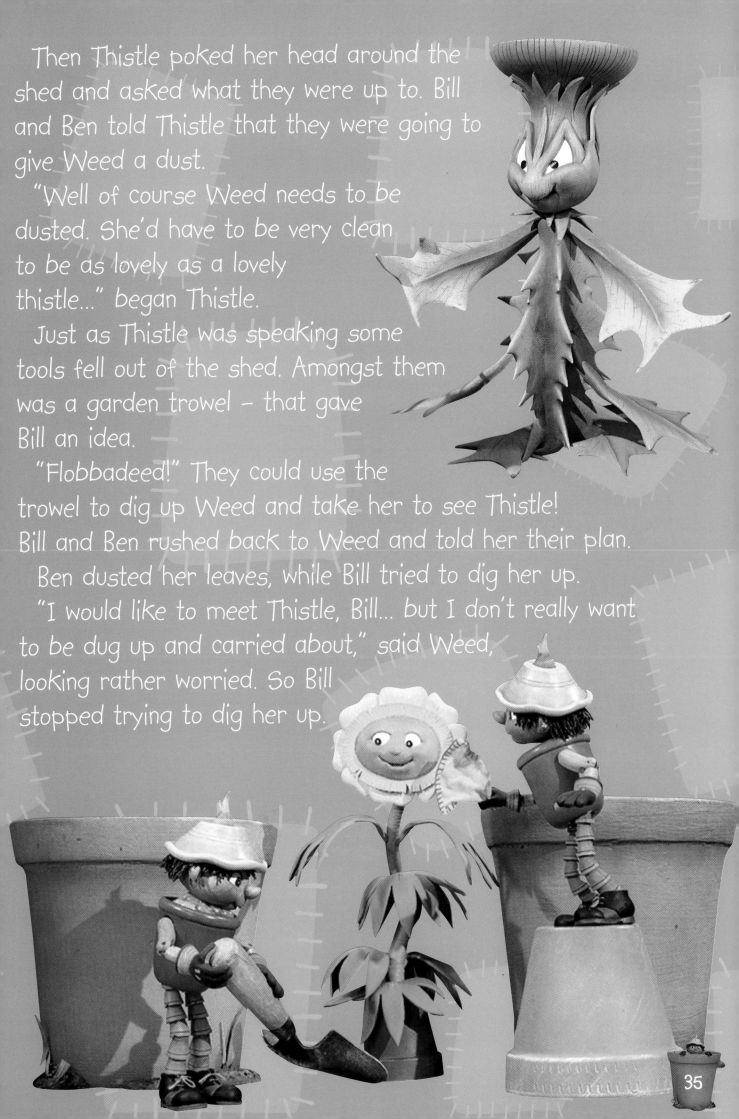

Then Thistle poked her head around the shed and asked what they were up to. Bill and Ben told Thistle that they were going to give Weed a dust.

"Well of course Weed needs to be dusted. She'd have to be very clean to be as lovely as a lovely thistle..." began Thistle.

Just as Thistle was speaking some tools fell out of the shed. Amongst them was a garden trowel – that gave Bill an idea.

"Flobbadeed!" They could use the trowel to dig up Weed and take her to see Thistle! Bill and Ben rushed back to Weed and told her their plan.

Ben dusted her leaves, while Bill tried to dig her up.

"I would like to meet Thistle, Bill... but I don't really want to be dug up and carried about," said Weed, looking rather worried. So Bill stopped trying to dig her up.

"I really would like to see what the rest of the world looks like. I've only ever seen our corner of the garden," sighed Weed, thoughtfully.

So Bill and Ben promised Weed that she would see the rest of the world. The trouble was, they didn't know how.

Soon, they bumped into Slowcoach who was out for a stroll.

"I only left home yesterday and already I've got as far as this sprout," he told them, feeling very proud.

"Flobbadurldaweed," said Ben.

"I should think Weed would like to see the world. But she is stuck in the ground. Hmm, that's a tricky one," said Slowcoach, trying to think of something. Suddenly, he had an idea.

"Got it! If Weed can't go to the world... the world must go to Weed!" Bill looked puzzled, so Slowcoach explained...

"We'll collect interesting things from around the world and show them to Weed!" he told them.

Bill and Ben thought this was an excellent idea. "Dobbaslobalob!" they cried and sped off to find some interesting things to show Weed.

First, Bill found Ketchup in the greenhouse. He showed Bill some interesting seed packets.

"They'll show Weed what goes on in a greenhouse," he said. So Bill collected up the seed packets and raced off.

Meanwhile, Ben was scooping up some mud to show Weed what a dirty part of the world looked like.

"Hee hee! Flubbadeed!" Ben was very pleased with himself.

Later on, Bill and Ben gave Weed their 'interesting things'. There was Ben's mud, Bill's seeds, an old trainer, a broken mug and a plastic clothes peg!

"Yes, these are all interesting things," said Weed. "There's just one tiny problem... I've seen all these things before, but I still don't know what the places they came from look like."

Suddenly Bill had an idea, "Flobbalicture!" he cried.

Weed understood. "Yes Bill, I'd know what they looked like if I saw a picture," she smiled.

Bill decided to use paints and hared off to find them while Bill went into Slowcoach's tunnel to find some pencils. Slowcoach gave Bill lots of pencils and plenty of paper. He decided to draw a picture of Rose, so off he went.

Meanwhile, Ben had found some paints, a brush and a roll of toilet paper to paint his pictures with. In fact when he pulled the roll of toilet paper it all unravelled and he had more paper than he could ever need!

Back in the garden, Bill was drawing Rose.

"I can't wait to see your drawing, Bill," she said, preening her petals. But when Bill turned his easel round to show Rose the picture, she wasn't very pleased!

"But it's nothing like me!" she cried. "I'm red and green, not grey," she sniffed.

Ben wasn't having much luck with his pictures either. Scamper thought he was drawing the compost heap, but it was actually the shed!

Later on, Bill and Ben took their pictures to show Slowcoach. But he wasn't very impressed.

"Dear me... My word... Oh dear," he sighed, looking at each of the pictures in turn.

"These pictures look nothing like the rest of the world!"

Bill and Ben felt rather miserable.

"Robbaflob," sighed Bill.

"Rubbaflub," sighed Ben.

"Never mind," said Slowcoach, "it was your first try."

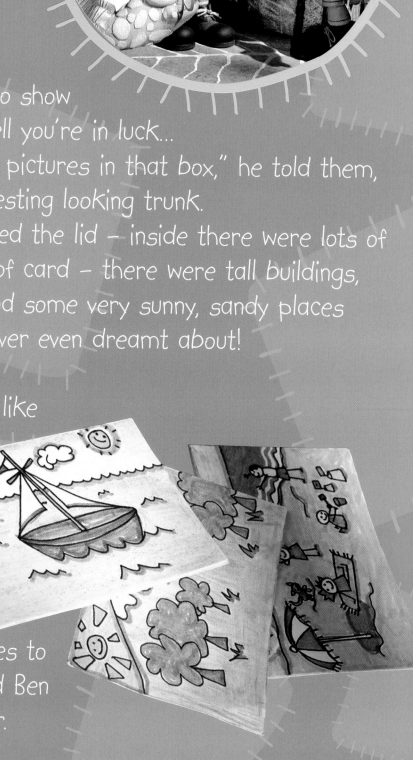

Luckily, Slowcoach had another idea.

"I know you promised to show Weed some pictures... well you're in luck... I have a fine collection of pictures in that box," he told them, nodding towards an interesting looking trunk.

Bill and Ben slowly opened the lid – inside there were lots of pictures on small pieces of card – there were tall buildings, huge ponds, mountains and some very sunny, sandy places which Bill and Ben had never even dreamt about!

"Flobbaled..." began Bill.

"I know they don't look like the vegetable patch or the garden shed, Bill. That's because they are pictures of the rest of the world!"

They were perfect pictures to show Weed, so Bill and Ben hurried off to show her.

They carefully laid out the postcards in front of Weed's pot so she could see them.

"They're all very lovely pictures, Bill and Ben. Very shiny," Weed began, thoughtfully.

"Rubbafluburld?" interrupted Ben.

Weed continued, "I'm pleased to see the world, Ben, but just look at all that snow and all that water... and all those people. Now I know what the world looks like, I'm very glad that I live in our own quiet corner of the garden."

Bill and Ben had showed Weed the world and they had to admit that they both agreed with her. They jumped up safely into their flowerpots and snuggled down as happy as could be.

To Bill, Ben and Weed there was no better place in the whole world than their very own corner of the garden.

Picture postcards

Bill and Ben showed Weed some postcards from around the world. Here are some other postcards from Slowcoach's collection – there i. writing on the back of them. Can you match the fronts to the backs?

Here's a picture of our hotel – look how snowy it is. Today I built a snowman!

xxx

PHEW!

Today we climbed to the top of this mountain!

xxx

Hello,
It's very warm and sunny here. I've been building sandcastles on the beach.
Wish you were here!

xxx

How does your garden grow?

Make a pretty garden on the page opposite, with pressed flowers, leaf and bark rubbings, just like Tashana's!

It's really easy to press flowers! Just put some petals in between paper (blotting paper is best). Place some heavy books on top and leave them there for a few weeks.

Make sure you use flowers from an old bouquet – don't pick the flowers.

Leaf and bark rubbings will make your picture look realistic. Just place a piece of paper over a dry leaf or tree bark and rub lightly over the top with a crayon or pencil. Cut it out and stick it onto your collage.

Now make your garden grow! Stick the dried flowers to the tops of the stalks. Add the rubbings to the tree. What else will you put in your garden?

Be Weed!

You can turn yourself into Little Weed with this great make!

1

Cut out a ring from yellow card – this should be big enough to fit around your face. Paper petals look just like Weed's petals. Glue these around the ring, just as Hayley is doing!

2

Cut out another ring of card, but this time cut into it to make a fringe – just like the one around Weed's face. Be careful though – don't go all the way through!

46

3

Finally, stick the fringe on top of the petals and you're ready to be Weed...

"How pretty!"

Gnome's puzzle corner

Look carefully at the pictures of Gnome below.
Can you spot the odd one out?

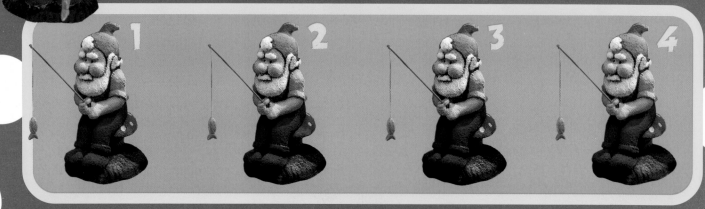

Use your crayons and pencils to brighten up Gnome.
Check the colour key below to make him look like his old self!

1
2
3
4
5
6
7

Look carefully at all the things in the pond.
Then answer the questions by writing true or false under each one.

There are 4 blue fish.

 False

Tad is sitting on a lily pad.

 true

There are 3 lily pads.

 False

There are 8 fish in total.

 true

Help Gnome to catch something on the end of his fishing line!
Draw a line from the rod to show what he's caught!

BEANS

Spot the difference

Who can you see in the picture? Finish the names below...

R_se

B_ll

B_n

There are four differences between these two pictures
– can you spot them all?

Write the differences here...

The windmill is DiFFerent

rose has a growing ross missing

there is a tree missing From the flower
pot

Flobbahats!

Turn yourself into Bill or Ben with these Flobbahats! You will need: a paper bowl, brown paint, brown and green tissue paper, safe glue, sticky tape

Bend up the edges of the paper bowl to make it look like the frill around Bill and Ben's hats. Glue the rim into place.

1

2

Paint the bowl brown and ask an adult to make a small hole in the centre of the hat.

3

Twist together some brown and green tissue paper to make a shoot just like Ben's!

4

Push the shoot into the hole at the top of the hat and your hat is ready to wear!

"Flobbadob!"

"Flubbadub!"

"Flobberly!"

Drainpipes and ladders

40 finish

39 Whizz down to number 22!

38

37

25

26

27

28 Follow Whimsy's web to number 30.

24

23 Climb up the flowerpot to number 26.

22

21

9

10

11 Catch a ride with Slowcoach. Miss a go.

12

8

7 Climb the ladder to number 9.

6

5 Climb the ladder to number 21.

Play Bill and Ben's fun up and down game with a friend. Take it in turns to roll a dice and move your counter across the board – buttons make great counters. If you land on a ladder, climb up, but if you land at the top of a drainpipe, down you go! There are other things to send you backwards or forwards too, so watch out!

36

35

34
Whizz down to number 19!

33
Thistle sends you back 3 spaces.

29
Climb the ladder to number 36!

30

31

32

Whizz down to number 3!

19

18

17

20

13

14

15
Climb the ladder to number 32!

16

4

3

2

1

Start

Tidy up!

There was a lot of scattered about the garden,

and was busily wriggling around collecting it to turn into

food for the . "Oh dear, oh dear, all this messy litter is

making the garden look untidy, it really is hard work collecting

it all!" he moaned, as another piece of flew out of his

mouth. "Flobbalobbaoops!" said , as he appeared with

They decided that needed some help. "Flubbalub!" said

Ben, picking up an old . "Ooooh, flobbalup," said Bill,

pulling a out of the bushes. It was no use though –

just when they'd piled up the rubbish, the wind blew it away

again!  plodded over when he heard the rustling of .

 litter
Whoops
plants

paper
Bill
apple

Ben

"Now, you know I'd love to help you out, but I'm not very quick on my toes..." he said. Soon,  appeared, offering a

helping paw. "I can gather the litter in my basket!" she said,

helpfully. But as soon as she put things in her basket, the wind

blew them out again!  came rushing past, impatiently.

"I say, could you give us a hand?" asked  . "Sorry, but

I'm far too busy to stop and chat," said Boo, curling up into a

prickly  and rolling away. But as Boo rolled around the

garden, he collected ALL the rubbish on his and he

didn't even know he was doing it!

"Robbadobbaboo!" cried Ben. Boo

had saved them a lot of hard work!

cup

Slowcoach

paper

Scamper

Boo

ball

prickles

Flubbaheehee!

Here are some of Bill and Ben's favourite jokes!

Q Which flowers are between your nose and your chin?
A Tulips! (Two lips!)

"Flubbaheehee!"

Q What do spiders do when they get angry?
A They go up the wall!

"Flobbahaha!"

Q Why did the fly fly?
A Because the spider spied her!

"Flubbaheehee!"

Q What time is it when an elephant sits on your flowerpot?
A Time to get a new flowerpot!

Flobbahaha!

Q Where do frogs keep their money?
A In a river bank!

Q How do you know which end of a worm is which?
A Tickle it in the middle and see which end laughs!

"Flubbaheehee!"

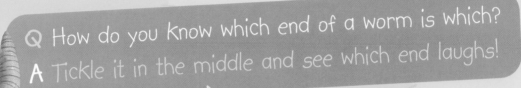

"Flobbahaha!"

Q What is a frog's favourite flower?
A A croakus!

"Flobbahaha!"

Q What time is it when the bell goes at Gnome School?
A Gnome time!

Bill and Ben have been HIDING inside your Annual. How many times can you find these pictures? They will be very small, so you'll have to look very closely!

Answer: Pages: 13, 19, 22, 28, 49, 53, 54.